FROM: TÍA ROSITA
USA
TO: SILVIA AND FAMILY
ANOTHER AMERICA

New Shoes for Silvia

SAN DIEGO
CA
AUG 20 '92

U.S. POSTAGE
$2.13
METER
9000953

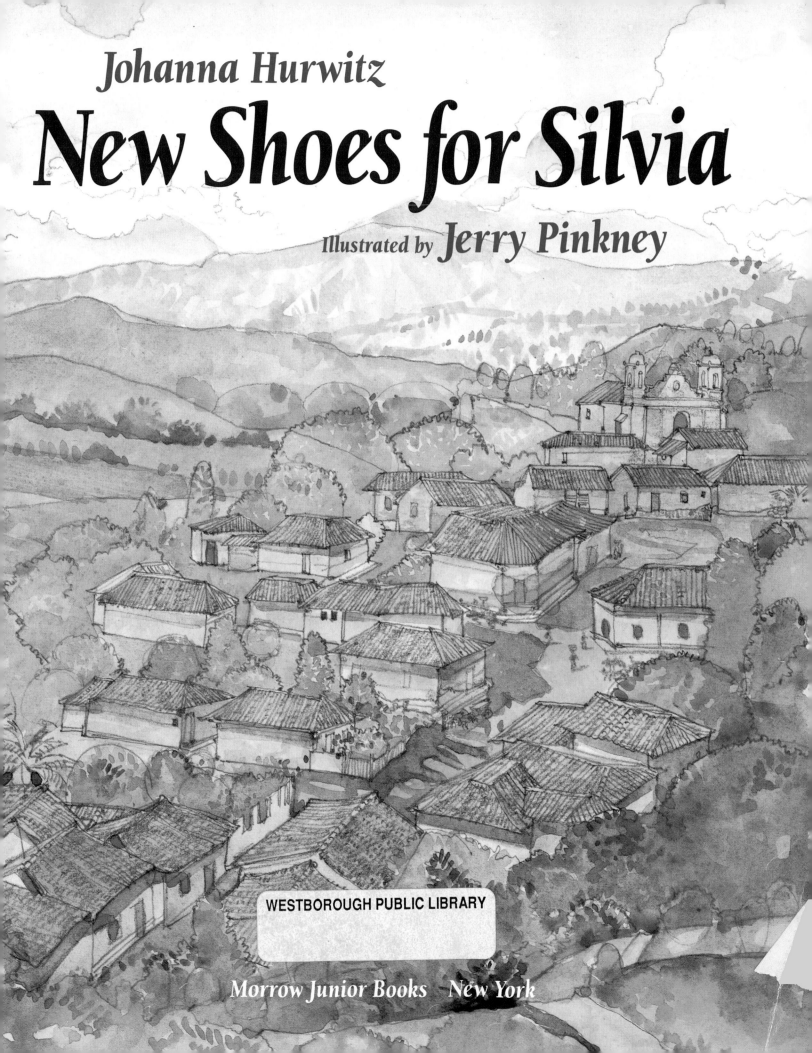

Johanna Hurwitz
New Shoes for Silvia

Illustrated by Jerry Pinkney

Morrow Junior Books   New York

The full-color artwork was done in pencil, Prismacolor, and watercolor on Arches watercolor paper.
The text type is 15-point Garamond Light.

Inquiries should be addressed to William Morrow and Company, Inc.,
1350 Avenue of the Americas, New York, NY 10019.
Printed in the United States of America.
1 2 3 4 5 6 7 8 9 10

Library of Congress Cataloging-in-Publication Data
Hurwitz, Johanna   New shoes for Silvia / by Johanna Hurwitz ; illustrated by Jerry Pinkney.   p.   cm.
Summary: A young girl receives a pair of beautiful red shoes from her Tía Rosita and finds different uses for them until she grows
enough for them to fit.
ISBN 0-688-05286-X. — ISBN 0-688-05287-8 (lib. bdg.)
[1. Shoes—Fiction. 2. Latin America—Fiction.] I. Pinkney,
Jerry, ill. II. Title. PZ7.H9574Nf 1993 [E]—dc20 92-40868 CIP AC

E
HUR

For Nomi and the children of Niquinohomo
—J. H.

To my grandson Rashad Cameron
—J. P.

Once, far away in another America, a package arrived at the post office. The package came from Tía Rosita. Inside there were gifts for the whole family.

For Silvia there was a wonderful present—a pair of bright red shoes with little buckles that shone in the sun like silver.

Right away, Silvia took off her old shoes and put on the beautiful new ones. Then she walked around so everyone could see.

"Mira, mira," she called. "Look, look."

"Those shoes are as red as the setting sun," her grandmother said. "But they are too big for you."

"Your shoes are as red as the inside of a watermelon," said Papa. "But they are too big. You will fall if you wear them."

"Tía Rosita has sent you shoes the color of a rose," said Mama. "We will put them away until they fit you."

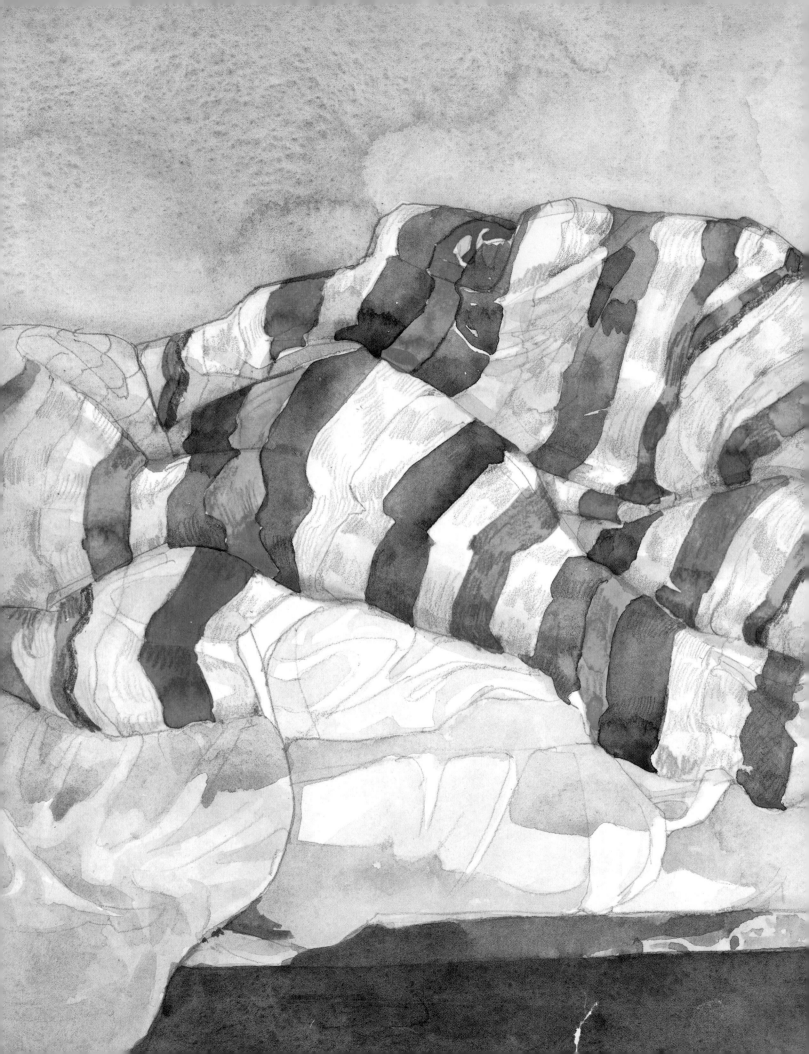

Silvia was sad. What good were new shoes if she couldn't wear them?

That night she slept with them in her bed.

The next morning Silvia put on the red shoes again. Perhaps she had grown during the night.

No. The shoes were still too big. But she saw that they were just the right size to make beds for two of her dolls. Even though it was morning, the dolls went right to sleep in their new red beds.

A week passed, and Silvia tried on the red shoes again. Perhaps she had grown during the week.

No. The shoes were still too big. But she saw that they made a fine two-car train. She pushed them all around the floor. What a good ride the babies had in their red train!

Another week passed, and Silvia tried on the red shoes again. Certainly by now she had grown big enough so they would fit.

No. The shoes were still too big. But Silvia found some string and tied it to the shoes. Then she pulled the shoes like oxen working in the field.

Still another week passed, and Silvia tried on the red shoes again. Would they fit now?

No. The shoes were still too big. But she saw that they were just the right size to hold the pretty shells and smooth pebbles that she had collected when she went to the beach with her grandparents.

Another week passed, and another and another. Sometimes Silvia was so busy playing with the other children or helping her mama with the new baby or feeding the chickens or looking for their eggs that she forgot to try on her new red shoes.

One day Mama wrote a letter to Tía Rosita. Silvia thought about the red shoes. She emptied out all the shells and pebbles and dusted the shoes off on her skirt. They were as red and beautiful as ever. Would they fit today?

Yes.

"*Mira, mira,*" she cried, running to show Mama and the baby. "Look, look. My shoes are not too big now."

Silvia wore her new red shoes when she walked to the post office with Mama to mail the letter.

"Maybe there will be a new package for us," said Silvia.

"Packages don't come every day," said Mama.

"Maybe next time Tía Rosita will send me new blue shoes," said Silvia.

They mailed the letter and walked home. Silvia's shoes were as red as the setting sun. They were as red as the inside of a watermelon. They were as red as a rose. The buckles shone in the sun like silver. And best of all, the shoes were just the right size for Silvia.